For David, Van, and Miss Truvy
—L. N.

For Zelka, Loki, and Baby Nikko
—E. O.

SIMON & SCHUSTER BOOKS FOR YOUNG READERS
An imprint of Simon & Schuster Children's Publishing Division
1230 Avenue of the Americas, New York, New York 10020
Text copyright © 2002 by Lesléa Newman
Illustrations copyright © 2002 by Erika Oller
SIMON & SCHUSTER BOOKS FOR YOUNG READERS is a trademark of Simon & Schuster.
Book design by Greg Stadnyk
The text of this book is set in 16-point Clearface.
The illustrations are rendered in watercolor.
Printed in Hong Kong
2 4 6 8 10 9 7 5 3 1
Library of Congress Cataloging-in-Publication Data
Newman, Lesléa.
Dogs, dogs, dogs! / by Lesléa Newman ; illustrated by Erika Oller.—1st ed.
p. cm.
Summary: A counting book featuring dogs engaged in various activities, from walking through the city all alone to slurping up a fallen ice-cream cone.
ISBN 0-689-84492-1
[1. Dogs—Fiction. 2. Counting. 3. Stories in rhyme.] I. Oller, Erika, ill. II. Title.
PZ8.3.N4655 Do 2002
[E]—dc21
00-068799

Dogs, Dogs, Dogs!

by
LESLÉA NEWMAN

illustrated by
ERIKA OLLER

Simon & Schuster Books for Young Readers

New York   London   Toronto   Sydney   Singapore

One dog walking through the city all alone

Two dogs chewing on
a big, delicious bone

Three dogs joining in
a pickup game of hoops

Four dogs climbing up
and down a row of stoops

Five dogs sneaking past a building full of cats

Six dogs wagging tails
at ladies wearing hats

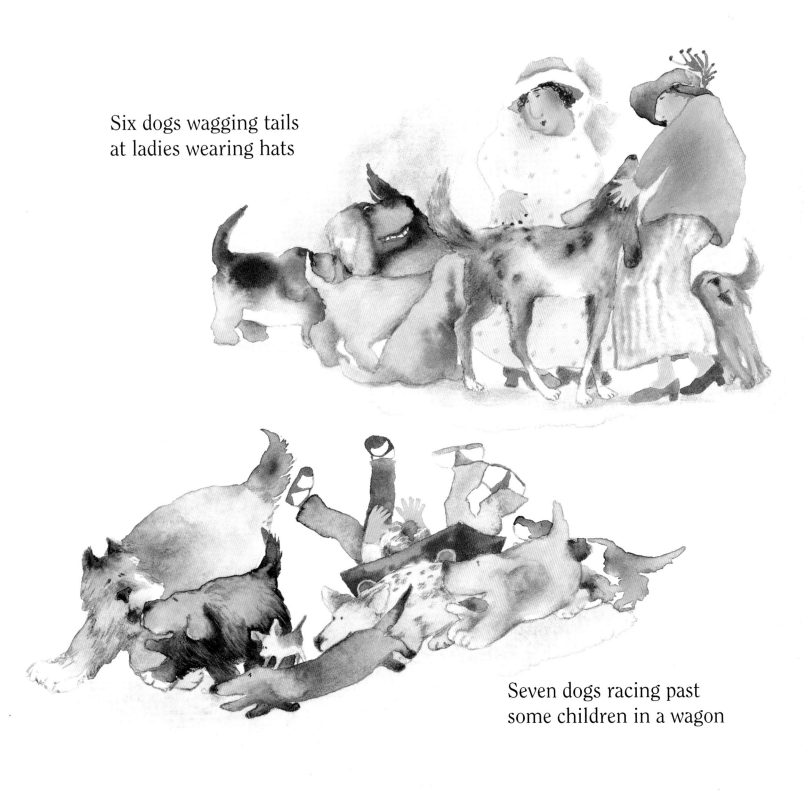

Seven dogs racing past
some children in a wagon

Eight dogs lunging at
a green and purple dragon

Nine dogs dashing through
a tunnel deep and dark

Ten dogs gallivanting right into the park

Dogs chasing tennis balls, dogs chasing sticks

Dogs chasing butterflies, dogs doing tricks

Dogs drinking out of puddles, dogs eating snacks

Dogs lying on their bellies, dogs on their backs

Dogs jumping in the lake,
dogs swimming laps

Dogs digging up the grass,
dogs taking naps

MIXED BREEDS

Dogs running here and there,
dogs all around

Dogs growing restless,
dogs homeward bound

Ten dogs strutting past a woman doing hair

Nine dogs posing for an artist in the square

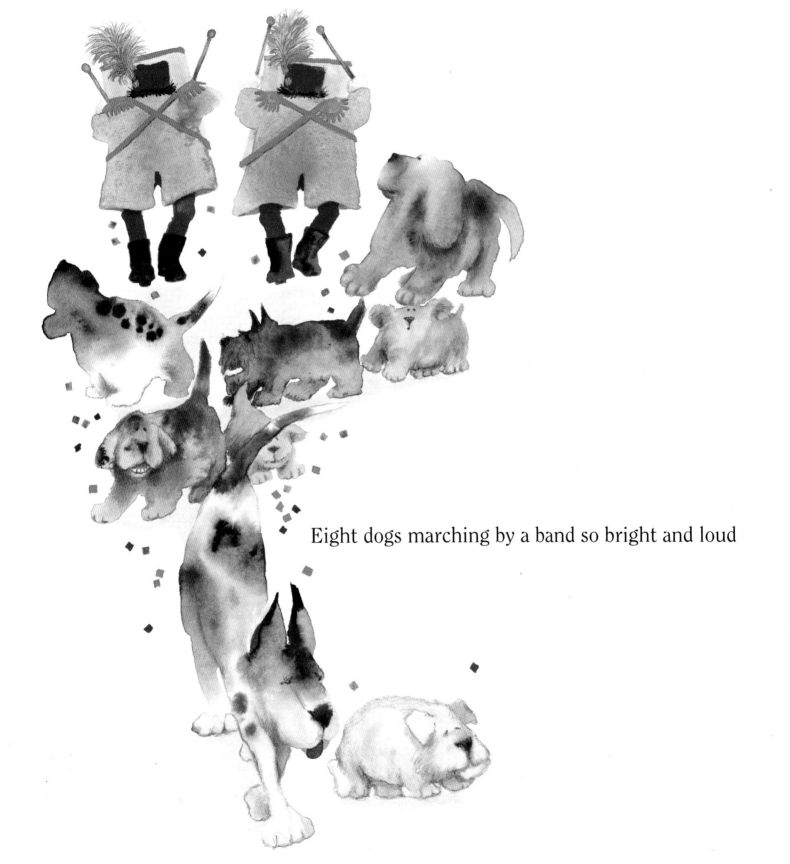

Eight dogs marching by a band so bright and loud

Seven dogs pushing through a most unruly crowd

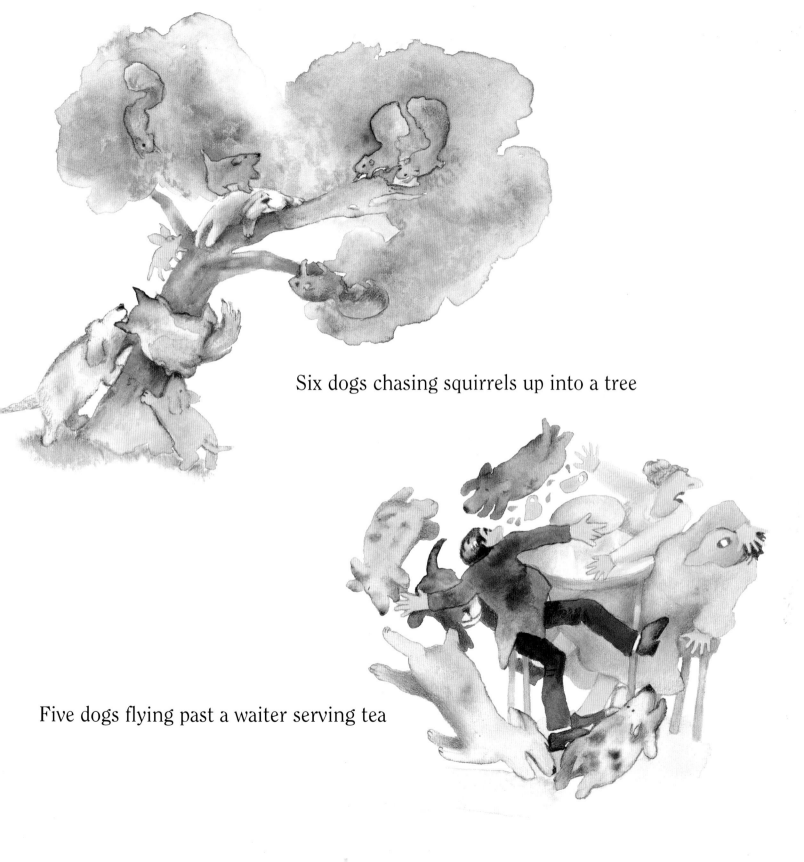

Six dogs chasing squirrels up into a tree

Five dogs flying past a waiter serving tea

Four dogs making traffic
honk, screech, and stop

Three dogs wandering into a pastry shop

Two dogs slurping up a fallen ice-cream cone

One dog walking through the city all alone